The best part of any test is leaving it behind!

Yeah -- until next week!

Do you **always** hafta piddle on my parade?

Find a table. I'll get the drinks.

Well...

...I kissed Dad good-bye when he went to work...

They don't mean **your own family**!

Hey, your father installed a computer filter. Did you bypass it?

...henh... actually... that's question 43...

Jesus said lust in your heart is the same as actual adultery.

There's a difference between a single stray thought and what Christ said.

Right! 'Cause if temptation or a single stray thought was a sin --

Whaddya say, J.C.?

Hasta la bye-bye, bozo!*

*Matthew 4:8-10 -- paraphrased -- Ed.

-- that would make Christ a sinner 'cause He was tempted!

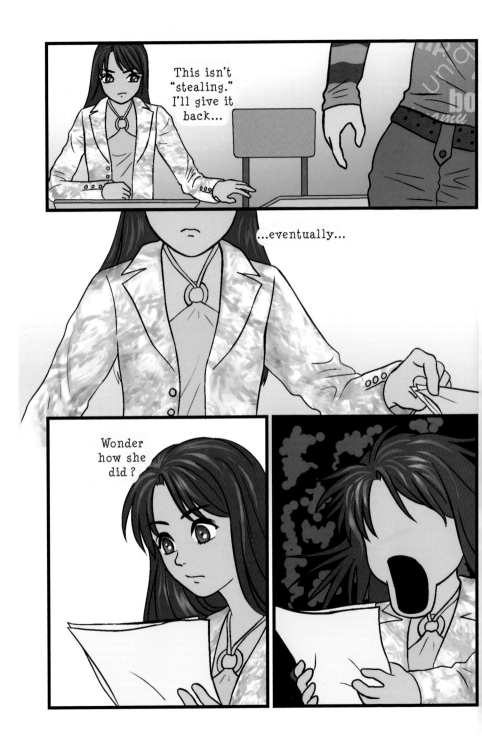

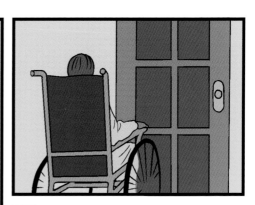

-- not
recklessly
or
promiscuously.

Yes,
ma'am.

Oh, and
one other
thing:

Turn
your computer
filter back
on.

Yes,
ma'am.

If the eggs **break** or you **lose** them --

SPlaはた

There's a **maniac** loose in the neighborhood!

What's Serenity's problem?

Want me to start listing them **alphabetically**?

Let's try that again...

Okay, let's see if we can get something in you!

=WAAAA!=

C'mon, open wide for Auntie Serenity...

Kimberly! Phone!

Coming, Mom!

Mood-wrecker...

Hey, Sally. What's up?

She **WHAT**?!?!?

...no... I couldn't do that...sorry ...no way...

On my.

What's up?

Apparently some kinda **trouble** over at Serenity's house.

Let me go with you. To...uh... help.

Police...?

Hey, you okay, Kimberly?

=unnnnnnnh=

Within minutes...

OH, NO!

ding dong

Did someone here call the police?

Back here, Officer Topp.

Forget it -- it's only an egg. This baby is real.

Not **this** meathead again!

(These two had a "run-in" in volume 2!)

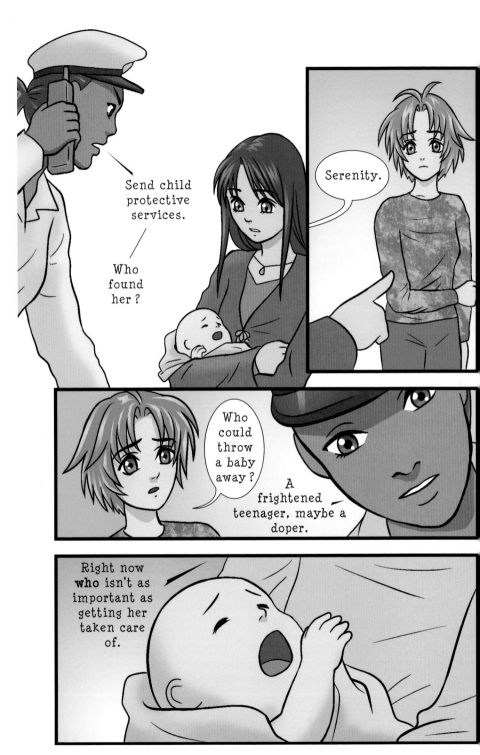

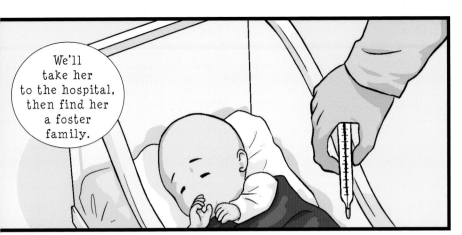

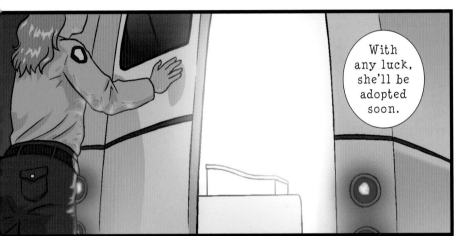

Life's a beach --
come and play!

"INSANELY
UNIQUE!"
-- *MangaPunk.com*

GOOFYFOOT GURL

You can find
anything on a beach
-- especially FUN
and ROMANCE!

Making her splash in Summer 2007!

Created by Realbuzz Studios
Published by Thomas Nelson
Find out more at
www.RealbuzzStudios.com

Wanna see?
Turn the page for a
SPECIAL SNEAK
PREVIEW!!!

THE revolve TOUR

Hawk Nelson

Natalie Grant

KJ-52

Max & Jenna Lucado

Ayiesha Woods

Chad Eastham

Kimiko Soldati

We're Coming to a City Near You!
TOUR DATES

Columbus, OH
September 14 - 15, 2007

Dallas, TX
September 21 - 22, 2007

Hartford, CT
September 28 - 29, 2007

St. Louis, MO
October 5 - 6. 2007

Anaheim, CA
October 12 - 13, 2007

Sacramento, CA
October 19 - 20, 2007

Philadelphia, PA
November 2 - 3, 2007

Minneapolis, MN
November 9 - 10, 2007

Portland, OR
November 16 - 17, 2007

Atlanta, GA
November 30 - Dec. 1, 2007

Orlando, FL
January 25 - 26, 2008

Charlotte, NC
February 1 - 2, 2008

Denver, CO
February 15 - 16, 2008

Houston, TX
February 22 - 23, 2008

Download
Preview Video
Online

To register by phone, call 877-9-REVOLVE
or online at REVOLVETOUR.COM

Serenity

Created by Realbuzz Studios, Inc.
Min Kwon, Primary Artist

Serenity throws a big wet sloppy one out to:
Hanna C., Jeannie L., Stephanie K., Darin F., Mike K.,
Maiolo and Melchman

Smack!
Luv U Guyz !!!

©&TM 2007 by Realbuzz Studios   ISBN 978-1-59554-385-1
www.Realbuzz Studios.com
www.SerenityBuzz.com

Published by Thomas Nelson, Inc. Nashville, TN 37214 www.thomasnelson.com

Library of Congress Cataloguing-in-Publication Data
Applied For

Scripture quotations marked NCV are taken from
The HOLY BIBLE, New Century VERSION®. NCV®.
Copyright © 2001 by Nelson Bibles.
Used by permission of Thomas Nelson. All rights reserved.

Printed in Singapore.
5 4 3 2 1

GOOFYFOOT GURL
hitting the beach this September!